MW00768419

# The GOLDEN HORSE

## An American Fairy Tale

*Story by*

# CATHERINE BRISTOW

*Illustrations by*

# C. BRUCE DUPREE

*10-23-96*
*To: The Students of*
*Barnett Shoals Elementary!*
*Follow your dreams!*
*— Catherine Bristow —*

**The Golden Horse: An American Fairy Tale.** Copyright © 1995 by Catherine Bristow. Printed and bound in Canada. All rights reserved. No part of this book may be reproduced in any form or by any electronic or mechanical means including information storage and retrieval systems without permission in writing from the publisher, except by a reviewer, who may quote brief passages in a review. Published by Nadan Publications, Columbus, Georgia. 2nd Printing

**Library of Congress Cataloging in Publication Data**

Bristow, Catherine
    The Golden Horse: An American Fairy Tale / by Catherine Bristow

ISBN 0-9645531-0-4

Distributed by Southern Publishers Group
(205) 250-8016
or Nadan Publications
(706) 568-0390

Printed in Canada

*Dedicated to:*

DANCES WITH WOLVES, MY FAMILY,

KIM FISHER—AND BRUCE,

WHO CAUGHT THE VISION OF MY STORY.

—CB

ONG, LONG AGO in the springtime of the year a daughter was born to parents who loved her dearly. They lived in a house by a winding river where the land abounded in growth. It seemed enchanted. There were rolling green hills, fields with wild flowers and forests filled with animals of many kinds. It was a time of plenty for this young family. It was a time of dear friends. It was a time of joy.

When the couple beheld the sight of their baby daughter, only one name came to mind. The name to capture the season into which she had been born—a symbol of the beauty that was exploding everywhere. The name chosen to radiate their love for her. April Rose.

April Rose grew strong by her parents' sides. She learned patience as she worked the land with them. She acquired respect as the earth bore its rewards, season after season. She became skilled in the ways of nature.

April Rose became beautiful as time passed. It was a beauty that blossomed from within. The games played with family and friends taught her to laugh. The stories they exchanged of the promise of the West excited her imagination. April's uncle, her father's youngest brother, encouraged her to dream with the tales he told of the wide open spaces, the silver in Nevada, the copper in Arizona. "Tell me again of your homestead," she would plead with twinkling eyes. He planned to move his family with the next wagon train.

April Rose eagerly elaborated upon her favorite stories when all was quiet and only her parents were near. "The wind blew the wild mustang's mane against the face of the girl as they raced across the prairie," the tale would begin. Sometimes her mother gathered drawing tools and sketched after these tales were told. A special part of April's story would come to life under her mother's pencils. They shared a creative trust.

One winter a fever spread through town. Her mother's friend became sick and she went to help. But during the days spent at her friend's side, her mother caught the fever. She returned home. April's father did all he could to make her get well again. But she never got better.

Her mother passed quietly from this life with her family at her side. April Rose and her father were devastated. April asked her father through quivering lips, "What will we do without her?" Her father held her close. He softly replied, "Your mother is part of nature now. She will be with us always." They laid her to rest in a peaceful place by the river. But he was overcome with anguish. So great was his sorrow that he died of a broken heart while mourning at her graveside.

April Rose was grief-stricken by the death of her parents. She felt lost. She would go to live with her aunt, her mother's only sister. It was hoped that family would help her to recover.

When it was time to leave home, April Rose kept just one possession—

the picture of a golden horse her mother had sketched for her.

Life at her aunt's house was quite different for April Rose. Her
aunt had two children, a girl close to April's age, Courtney, and a boy
several years younger, Bradley. They were jealous of the good-natured
April Rose. Her cousins shunned her. They did not include her in the
family activities. Her aunt made little time for April as she involved
herself in her own family. She made April Rose tend to the animals
and tasks on the farm. "You will earn your keep."

Each day saw April rising to feed the animals. Although there was much to do, it was her favorite part of the day. As she cared for them, the animals grew to love her. They made her feel special again. They reminded her to dream. While she worked, they listened quietly when she lost herself in stories remembered from long ago. "They raced through the canyon stream, water spraying in all directions..." she would begin.

Her aunt demanded that the yard be kept neat. Day after day, the dirt around the house had to be raked in fine wavy lines. Week after week, weeds were never to be in the garden or flower bed. Month after month, the wood was to be kept stacked. Season after season, the ripened vegetables were to be gathered or a garden plot to be prepared.

Planting seeds

Chopping firewood

Weeding the garden

*Washing clothes (the worst.)*

*Peeling Apples*

*Cleaning floors*

The household chores were endless: scrubbing floors, dusting furniture, beating rugs, laundry. But April Rose had learned the value of work from her parents, so she did these things without complaint. She had also learned to dream from her parents.

At night, the responsibilities of the day behind her, April Rose would retire to her small room above the kitchen. When she lay in bed she would gaze at the drawing, the gift from her mother. Her imagination would take her away from the farm, away from the work, away from the hurt.

April could see the beloved horse in all her majesty. The wind blowing her mane as she stood atop a hill, head held high, ears pricked forward as she looked for April Rose. There was only one name that came to mind. The name to capture the horse's beauty and power—to symbolize her freedom. The name taken from stories retold from long ago. Golden Grace.

The animals of her aunt's farm knew Golden Grace. April Rose often told them her adventures with the palomino. The animals were always attentive as the stories came to life: daring escapes, racing the wind, rescuing the forest creatures, quiet canters toward her uncle's homestead in Arizona. They were a team, April Rose and Golden Grace.

Sometimes when her cousins overheard April talking to the animals they would tease her. Courtney and Bradley could be very mean. They would mock her and pretend to hurt the precious horse of her dreams. April Rose would try to ignore them but it was very difficult.

One day as April was gathering vegetables from the garden, Courtney and Bradley came over. Courtney asked April Rose to tell her more of the horse adventures. April Rose hesitated, trying instead to think of other things to say. But they began to taunt her, to make fun of her. "Oh please take me away from here, dear horse. My cousins don't like me," they whined.

Pinecone

Star Quilt

c. 1885
Summer Rose

Bradley started throwing tomatoes. One tomato hit April Rose and, without thinking, she threw an ear of corn at him. It missed but more tomatoes did not. She continued throwing corn at him as she tried to get away.

Her aunt heard the commotion and came to the garden. Courtney quickly placed all the fault on April Rose. Bradley, who had bitten his own arm, showed his mother what "April" had done. Her aunt was furious. She blamed the ruined corn, the trampled garden, the entire fight on April Rose. And then Courtney did one thing more.

She told her mother of the golden horse. She told of April's daydreaming that kept her from her work. She told of the stories that April Rose used to "tease" the animals. She reminded her mother of the picture on the wall.

April Rose watched in horror as her aunt stormed to the room above the kitchen and took down the framed picture. She ripped the beloved horse into small pieces of paper as April looked on in wide-eyed disbelief.

April Rose stumbled backward. She knew it was time to go. There was no real place for her here, not any more. Her parents would not have wanted it this way. The tears flowed down her cheeks as she ran from the house, ran as far as she could, ran until she collapsed on the grassy hillside. Utterly exhausted, she surrendered to sleep.

A few hours later, April Rose was awakened by a quiet, familiar sound. There she stood. Golden Grace. Her mane was blowing lightly in the wind, her ears were pricked forward and she had found April Rose.

April caught her breath in wonder when the beloved horse nickered a soft greeting. April's arms found the golden horse's neck. She buried her face in the flaxen mane as the tears came once again—tears of relief, of joy, of freedom. April Rose rode Golden Grace far, far away as they raced the wind. They headed west toward Arizona. A new life had begun.

The Golden Horse
Bristow, Catherin